HANS CHRISTIAN ANDERSEN

English text
by ANNE
STEWART

The Ugly Duckling

Illustrated by

MONIKA LAIMGRUBER

Greenwillow Books,
New York

It was summer and the countryside was beautiful. The wheat was golden yellow, the oats were green, and in the meadows the hay was gathered into bales. Around the fields and meadows there were large forests, and in the middle of these forests deep lakes. To be sure, the countryside looked very beautiful indeed.

An old house stood bathed in the sunlight. It was surrounded by a deep moat, and between the house and the moat grew giant coltsfoot leaves. They were so tall that a young child could stand upright beneath them. Among the leaves, it was as overgrown and wild as the thickest wood.

A duck sat on her nest. She was waiting for her ducklings to hatch, but she was growing impatient because she had been there for a long time and hardly anyone had come to see her. The other ducks preferred to swim around in the moat than come and chat with her under a leaf.

But, at last, one egg cracked open and the baby duckling cheeped loudly. Then other ducklings burst through their shells and poked their heads into the air. Their mother quacked and they shook themselves free from their shells and scurried among the green leaves, looking all around them.

"How big the world is," said the ducklings, who now had much more room to move than they had had in their shells.

"Don't think this is the whole world," said their mother. "It stretches much farther than this. It goes right up to the other side of the garden and into the vicar's fields – though I

haven't ever been that far myself. Are you all here?"

Then she saw that the biggest egg was still lying in the nest. "How much longer is this going to take?" she sighed. "I've just about

had enough!" And she sat down on the egg again.

Just then, an old duck arrived. She had come to visit the mother duck.

"How's it going?" she asked.

"This last egg is taking such a long time," replied the mother duck. "It just won't hatch. But do look at my other ducklings. They are the sweetest things I've ever seen. They're just like their father, the bad creature. He hasn't come to see me yet."

"Show me an egg that won't hatch," said the old duck, "and I'll show you a turkey egg. I was taken in the same way once and I had the most terrible time. Turkeys are afraid of water, you know. I couldn't get him to go in. I quacked at him and snapped at him, but it didn't make any difference. Let me see the egg." She looked at it and then said, "Well, there's no doubt about it. It's a turkey egg all right. I'd leave it and take the other ducklings swimming if I were you."

"I'll sit on it just a bit longer," said the mother duck. "I've sat on it so long already, a few minutes more won't make any difference." "It's up to you," said the old duck, and she waddled away.

At last, the egg hatched. Cheeping loudly, the baby duckling burst through his shell. He was very large and very ugly. The mother duck looked at him. "He's terribly big for a duckling," she said to herself. "None of the others looked like that. Perhaps he *is* a turkey. Well, I'll soon find out. I'll get him into the water, even if I have to push him in."

The next day, the weather was again beautiful and the sun shone brightly on the coltsfoot plants. The mother duck and her family walked to the edge of the moat. The mother duck

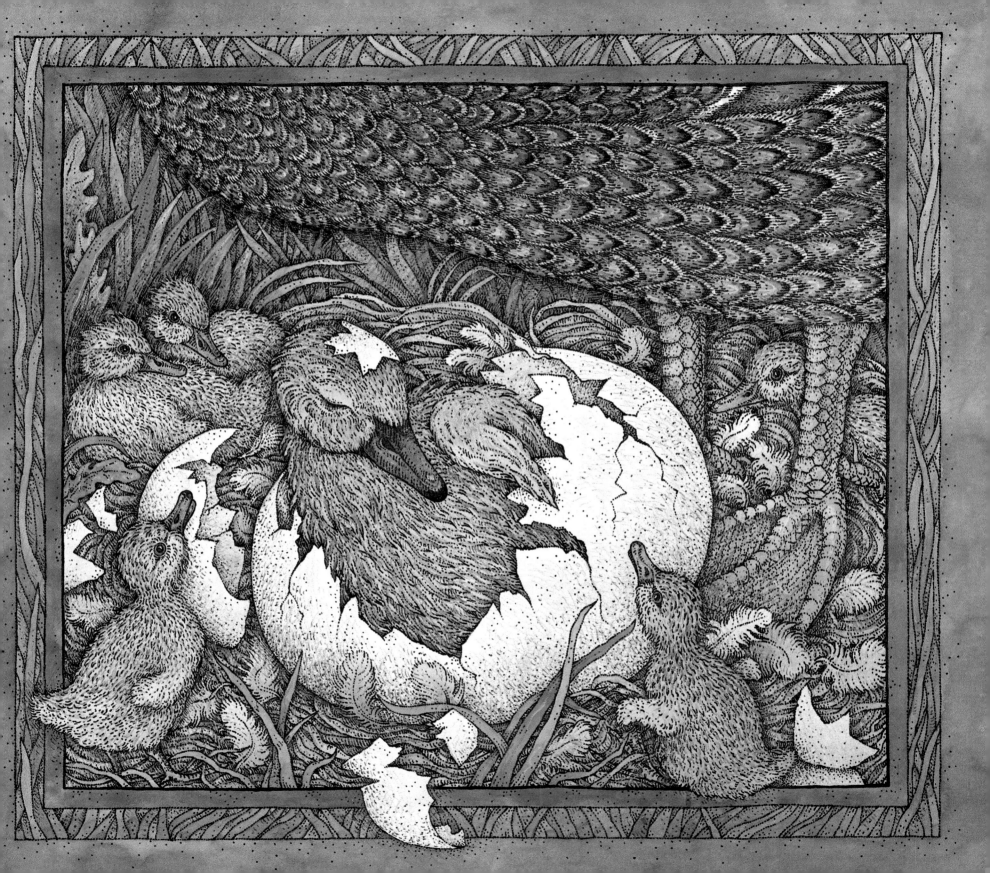

jumped into the water with a splash. "Quack, quack," she said and the ducklings followed her in, one after the other. They all disappeared under the water, but immediately bobbed up again and swam away quite expertly. Even the ugly, dirty-grey duckling swam with ease.

"He can't be a turkey," thought the mother duck. "He paddles quite beautifully and he holds himself very straight. He must be mine. And, in fact, he's quite handsome if you look at him properly." Quacking loudly, she called the ducklings to her side. "Come with me now and I'll take you into the world and introduce you to the ducks in the duckyard. But stay close and look out for the cat!"

A short time later, they arrived at the duck-
yard. It was terribly noisy because two families were fighting over an eel's head. Then the cat snatched the head and carried it off. "How typical!" sighed the mother duck, and then sighed again because she too would have liked the eel's head. "Now, hurry up," she said. "Make sure you bow to the old lady duck over there. She's the most important duck here. Her family originally came from Spain, which explains why she is rather plump. As you can see, she has a piece of red cloth tied around her leg. This is the highest honour a duck can receive, and it means that everybody knows how very important she is. Hurry up! Don't turn your feet in. A well brought up duck points its feet outwards, just like your mother and father do. Watch me! Now, bow your head and say *Quack!*"

They obeyed. But the other ducks, who had been watching them, said loudly, "Oh dear, oh dear! Are we going to have them hanging round our necks? As if there weren't enough of us already. And just look at that one! We don't want him here!" And one of the ducks flew up to the ugly duckling and nipped him on the back of his neck.

"Stop it!" said the mother duck. "He's not doing any harm."

"No. But he's too big, and he looks very odd," said the duck who had nipped him. "He must be taught a lesson."

"All your other children are very good-looking," said the duck with the piece of cloth around her leg. "But this one hasn't turned out properly. It's a pity he hatched at all."

"That's not fair, your grace," said the mother duck. "He isn't handsome, but he has a very kind nature and he swims just as well as any of his sisters – in fact, rather better. I think his looks will improve when he's older. It's just that he was in the egg too long and so he's now a bit out of shape." And she nuzzled his neck and smoothed his feathers. "What's more, he's a male duck," she added "and there aren't many of them about. I think he's going to be really

duckling, and even his brothers and sisters were unkind to him. "If only the cat would get you, you horrible thing," they said. The hens pecked him and the girl who brought the food, lashed out at him with her foot.

At last, the ugly duckling decided to run

strong one day, quite an exceptional duck." The old duck only said, "Your other children are charming. Do make yourself at home – and if you happen to come across an eel's head I would be happy to accept it."

And so the mother duck and her ducklings were welcomed into the duckyard – all except the duckling who had been the last to hatch and was so ugly. "He's much too big," the ducks and hens all said. And the turkey cock, who had been born with spurs and so considered himself superior to all the other birds, puffed himself up and, like a ship under full sail, went up to the duckling and became so angry his face turned quite red. The poor duckling didn't know what to do or where to go, and he was sad because he was so ugly and everybody laughed at him.

The first day passed, and from then on each new day was worse than the one before. The ducks and hens went on teasing the poor little

away. He flew over the fence and the small birds in the bushes fluttered up in alarm. "They did that because I'm so ugly," thought the duckling, and he shut his eyes – though he didn't stop running! Then, at last, he came to a marsh where the wild ducks lived. Feeling tired and unhappy, he lay down and fell asleep.

The next morning, the wild ducks flew up to the new arrival and looked closely at him. "What kind of duck are you?" they asked. The duckling turned towards them and tried to answer. "You're terribly ugly," said the wild ducks. "But that doesn't matter as long as you don't marry into our family." Poor little duckling! He hadn't even thought of getting married. All he wanted was to be allowed to lie in the reeds and drink a bit of water.

He stayed in the marsh for two whole days. Then two wild geese came along. They were both young, male and rather cheeky. "Listen here, old chap," they said. "You're so ugly we've taken quite a fancy to you. Why don't you come with us and see the world? There's another marsh quite near here where some good-looking females live. You're so ugly you might just strike lucky!"

But at that moment two shots rang out and both geese fell into the marsh dead. The water turned blood red. Bang, bang. More shots were fired and a whole flock of geese flew up out of the reeds. A big hunt had started and the hunters were positioned all round the edge of the marsh; some even sat in the trees overlooking it. Blue clouds of smoke drifted among the branches and hung above the water over a wide distance. The hunting dogs splashed through the mud and flattened the reeds.

The poor little duckling was very frightened and had just turned his head to put it under his wing, when he got a terrible shock. A huge dog was standing in front of him, his eyes glittering and his tongue lolling out of his mouth. He lowered his jaw over the duckling, bared his sharp teeth – and then splashed away, leaving the duckling alone. "Thank goodness," said the duckling and he heaved a sigh of relief. "I'm so ugly the dog didn't want to bite me." And he lay quite still while the shots whistled through the reeds.

As the day wore on, everything gradually became quiet, but still the poor duckling didn't dare move. But, at last, he stood up, quickly looked around, and then hurried out of the marsh as fast as his legs would carry him. He crossed field after field, fighting against the wind

which was blowing so strongly he could hardly go on. Then, towards evening, he arrived at a ramshackle little cottage, so rickety it couldn't decide which wall should collapse first – and so it still stood up. The wind was now blowing so hard the duckling had to sit down to stop himself being blown away. Then the duckling noticed that the door of the cottage had come loose from its hinges and that there was a gap between the door and the wall. He slipped through it and

went inside.

An old lady lived in the cottage with her cat and her hen. The cat, whom she called Sonny, could hump his back and purr; he could also hiss, but he only did this if you stroked his fur the

wrong way. The hen had very short legs and so was called Sally Shortlegs. She laid good eggs and the old woman loved her like her own child.

The next morning, they noticed the duckling

straight away. The cat began to purr and the hen started to cluck. "What's this then?" said the old woman, because she couldn't see very well and thought the duckling was a plump female duck that had got lost. "This is a bit of luck. Now I can have duck eggs too – unless it's a male duck of course. We'll have to wait and see." But after three weeks no eggs had been laid.

The cat was master in the house and the hen, the mistress. They thought they were better than anyone else in the world. The duckling said opinions about this could differ, but the hen

"What on earth are you talking about?" she said. "Just because you haven't got anything to do, you get these fads into your head. Lay eggs or purr, then they will go away."

"But swimming is so marvellous," said the duckling. "It's so nice to put your head under-water and dive to the bottom."

"That must be great fun," said the hen with a sneer. "You're going crazy. Ask the cat, the cleverest creature I know, whether he thinks there's anything in swimming or diving. Or just ask the old lady. She's the wisest person in the

wouldn't hear of such a thing.

"Can you lay eggs?" she asked.

"No."

"Then keep quiet." And the cat asked,

"Can you hump your back or purr or hiss?"

"No."

"In that case you can't have any opinions about what clever people say."

The duckling sat in the corner and was sad. Then he started to think of the fresh air and the sunshine. He wanted to swim so much he had to tell the hen about it.

world. Do you think she likes swimming and getting her head wet?"

"You don't understand," said the duckling.

"Who will, if we don't?" replied the hen. "Leaving myself out of this, you won't find anyone cleverer than the cat or the old lady. Don't make such a fuss! Be thankful for everything that's been done for you. Here you are in a warm room with people you can learn something from. What more could you want? But you're a fool, and no fun to live with. Believe me, I'm only saying this for your own good;

that's the way to recognise your true friends. Just concentrate on laying eggs or learn how to purr or hiss."

"I'm going to go out into the big wide world," said the duckling. "You do that," said the hen.

And so he did. He swam and dived, but all the other animals ignored him because he was so ugly.

Then the autumn came. The leaves in the wood turned yellow, then brown, and the wind tossed them into the air so that they seemed to dance. The clouds became swollen with snow and a lone crow stood on a fence and cawed in the frosty air. It was hard for the poor little duckling.

One evening, when there was a glorious sunset, a flock of beautiful large birds came out from the undergrowth. The duckling had never seen such exquisite creatures before. They were brilliant white and had long, supple necks. Spreading their powerful wings, they uttered strange mournful cries and soared high into the sky to begin their journey to warmer lands across the sea. The duckling thought they were the most wonderful creatures he had ever seen. Stretching his neck out towards them, he emitted a cry so unearthly that he himself was frightened by it.

As soon as the birds were out of sight, the duckling dived to the bottom of the lake. When he came up again, he was quite overcome. He didn't know what the birds were called or where they were flying to, but from that moment he loved them more than he had loved anything ever before. He didn't envy them. It didn't occur to him to desire such perfection for himself. He would have been quite happy just to have been accepted by the ducks. Poor, ugly duckling.

Then winter came and it grew even colder. The duckling had to swim round and round to stop the water from freezing, but every night the hole he swam in grew smaller. He had to move his legs all the time to stop the hole from freezing over. But, at last, he became so exhausted that

he lay quite still and froze completely in the ice.

The next morning a farmer who was passing by saw the duckling. He went out onto the ice and used his wooden shoe to smash through the ice round the duckling to free him. Then he carried him home to his wife. There the duckling came slowly back to life.

The farmer's children wanted to play with the

other to catch the duckling. Luckily, the door was open. The duckling rushed outside and scuttled into the bushes. He lay in the freshly fallen snow, as though dead.

It would be too sad to describe all the difficulties and hardships the duckling had to suffer during that long hard winter. Let's just say that

duckling, but he thought they wanted to hurt him. In his fright, he knocked over a pitcher of milk and the milk splashed all over the room. The farmer's wife screamed and clapped her hands, so that the duckling flew into the butter dish and then into the flour barrel. What a mess! The farmer's wife screamed again and tried to hit the duckling with the fire tongs. The children laughed and shouted and tumbled over each

he was in the marsh, lying among the reeds, when the sun began to shine warmly again and when the larks started to sing. It was the start of a glorious spring.

The duckling flew into the air and his wings carried him faster and farther than they had ever done before. In no time at all, he found himself in a large garden. Here, the apple trees were in blossom and lilacs perfumed the air, hanging down from their long green branches to the moat below. Everything was so beautiful, so full of new life.

In front of the duckling were three magnificent white swans. Ruffling their feathers, they glided effortlessly towards him. The duckling recognised them and was overcome with sadness. "If I dare to approach these beautiful birds, they will kill me because I'm so ugly," he said. "But I don't care! I prefer to be killed than tormented by the ducks and hens, or kicked by the girl in the duckyard, or forced to endure another hard winter."

And so the duckling flew down to the water and swam towards the swans. They saw him and bore down upon him, rustling their feathers. "Kill me!" cried the poor duckling, and he lowered his head and waited for death. But what did he see? Looking down into the clear water, he saw his reflection. He wasn't a clumsy, ugly, dirty-grey bird any longer – he was a swan!

The other swans swam around the young swan and nuzzled him with their beaks. Just then, some small children came into the garden.

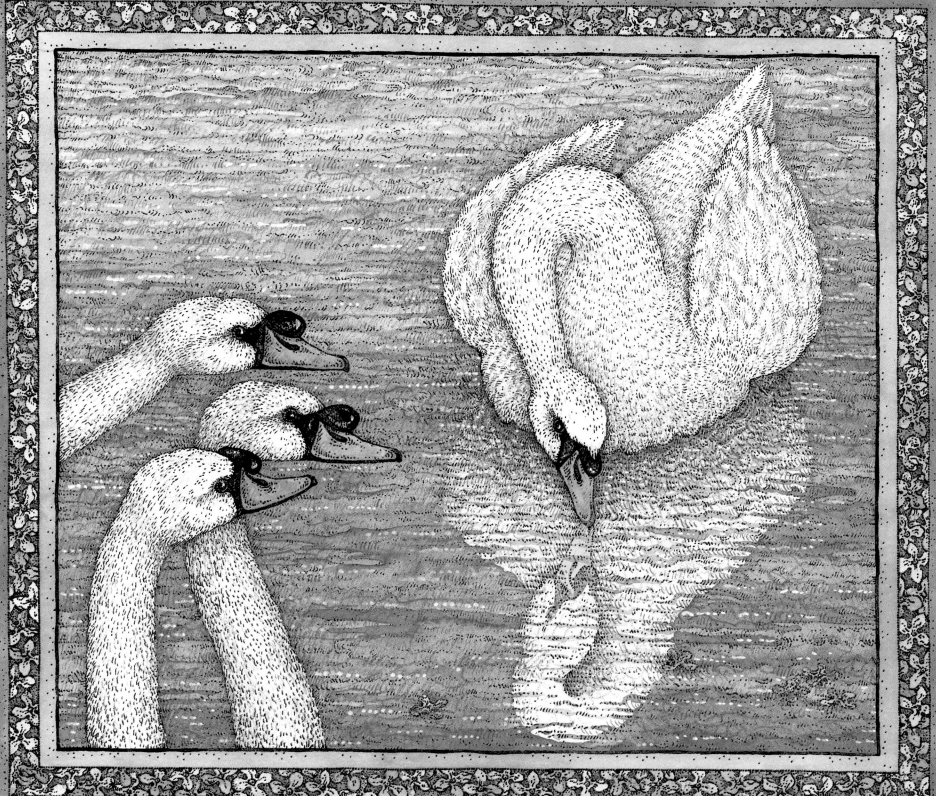

They threw breadcrumbs into the water, and the youngest child said, "Look! There's a new swan!" And the other children clapped their hands for joy and called out to the grown-ups, "A new swan's arrived!" They threw more bread and pieces of cake into the water. "The new one's the prettiest," they all said. "He's so young and beautiful." And the other swans bowed before him.

The young swan felt embarrassed and put his head under his wing. He was so happy, he could hardly bear it. He remembered how he had been persecuted and teased – and how he was now called the most beautiful of birds. But he wasn't proud, for a good heart is never proud. And the lilacs bent their branches towards him and the sun caressed him with its warmth. The young swan ruffled his feathers, stretched out his slim neck and felt a deep joy in his heart: "Never did I dream of such happiness when I was an ugly duckling," he said.

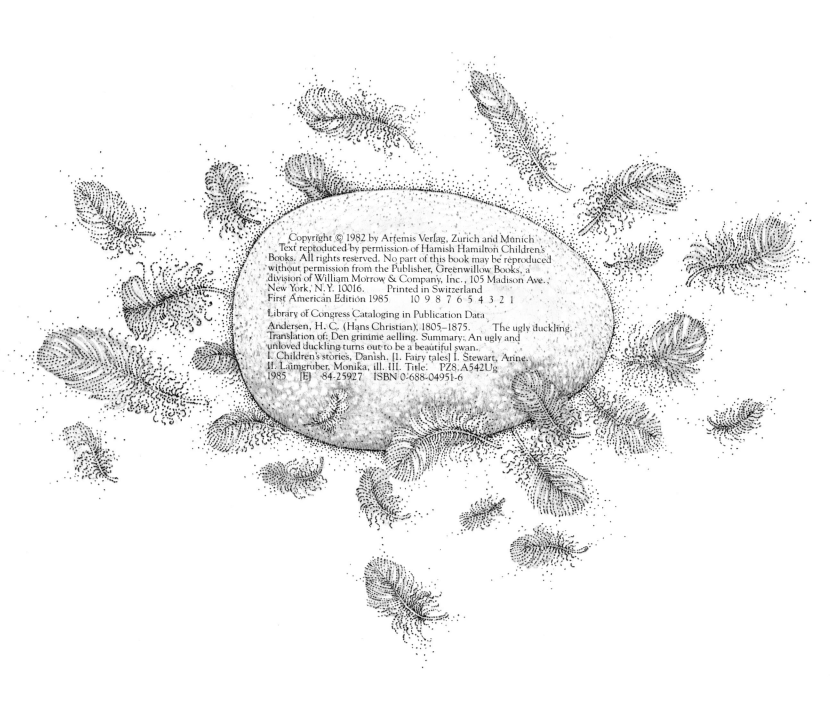

First American Edition 1985   10 9 8 7 6 5 4 3 2 1

Library of Congress Cataloging in Publication Data
Andersen, H. C. (Hans Christian), 1805–1875.   The ugly duckling.
Translation of: Den grimme aelling. Summary: An ugly and
unloved duckling turns out to be a beautiful swan.
I. Children's stories, Danish. [1. Fairy tales] I. Stewart, Anne.
II. Laimgruber, Monika, ill. III. Title.   PZ8.A542Ug
1985   [E]   84-25927   ISBN 0-688-04951-6